Rabbit
MOONCAKES

Written and Illustrated by

HOONG YEE LEE KRAKAUER

Little, Brown and Company
Boston New York Toronto London

For Seth, Mikki Lee, Remy Lee,
and, of course, Hoong Wei

First Edition

Library of Congress Cataloging-in-Publication Data
Krakauer, Hoong Yee Lee.
  Rabbit mooncakes / written and illustrated by Hoong Yee Lee Krakauer.
— 1st ed.
      p.   cm.
  Summary: A little Asian American girl overcomes her fear of family piano recitals.
  ISBN 0-316-50327-4
  [1. Piano — Performance — Fiction.   2. Fear — Fiction.   3. Asian Americans —
Fiction.]
  I. Title.
PZ7.K8586Rab   1994   92-23409
[E] — dc20

10 9 8 7 6 5 4 3 2 1

SC

Published simultaneously in Canada
by Little, Brown & Company (Canada) Limited

Printed in Hong Kong

Chinese calligraphy by the author's mother, Ming Hwa Hsiung Lee

Author's Note

As children growing up among the tall red-brick buildings near New York City, my sister Hoong Wei and I spent many summer hours nestled in the leafy branches of a crab apple tree. It was a treasured place for us; there, between the grass and sky, we spoke a mixture of English, Mandarin (from my mother's side), and Cantonese (from my father's side). It was our own funny language, which only she and I understood.

At the end of each summer, we celebrated our favorite holiday, the Harvest Moon Festival. On this Chinese version of Thanksgiving, under the fullest and brightest moon of the year, my entire family would gather to eat sweet golden harvest mooncakes, sing Chinese poem songs, and make our annual toasts to the lucky Harvest Moon. On one particular Harvest Moon Festival, in the Year of the Rabbit, I came to believe that this special Chinese holiday would always bring good luck to me and my family, throughout the year.

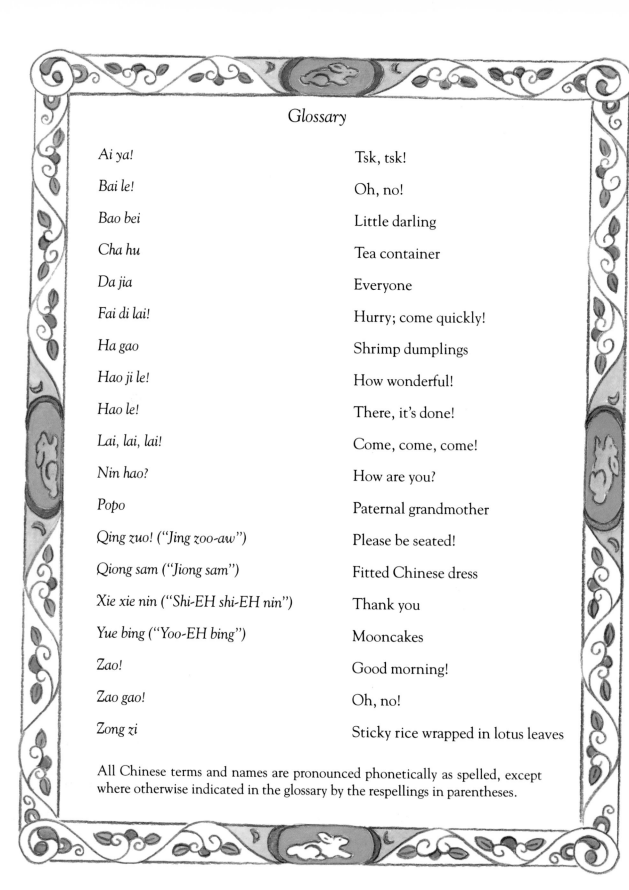

Glossary

Ai ya!	Tsk, tsk!
Bai le!	Oh, no!
Bao bei	Little darling
Cha hu	Tea container
Da jia	Everyone
Fai di lai!	Hurry; come quickly!
Ha gao	Shrimp dumplings
Hao ji le!	How wonderful!
Hao le!	There, it's done!
Lai, lai, lai!	Come, come, come!
Nin hao?	How are you?
Popo	Paternal grandmother
Qing zuo! ("Jing zoo-aw")	Please be seated!
Qiong sam ("Jiong sam")	Fitted Chinese dress
Xie xie nin ("Shi-EH shi-EH nin")	Thank you
Yue bing ("Yoo-EH bing")	Mooncakes
Zao!	Good morning!
Zao gao!	Oh, no!
Zong zi	Sticky rice wrapped in lotus leaves

All Chinese terms and names are pronounced phonetically as spelled, except where otherwise indicated in the glossary by the respellings in parentheses.

"*Lai, lai, lai!*" Hoong Yee and Hoong Wei heard their mother call out from the side door. "Come here, please!"

The two sisters climbed down the shady crab apple tree and raced into the kitchen, where each morning Mama combed their shiny black hair into pigtails.

"Aren't you girls lucky!" said Mama, twisting Hoong Yee's long hair into two smooth tassels. "I am going to put new red ribbons in your hair for tonight's Harvest Moon Festival."

Red, Hoong Wei knew, brought good luck. And so did a full moon. Perhaps she would be especially lucky tonight.

"Mama," she said hopefully as she climbed up for her turn, "maybe we shouldn't play the piano for everyone tonight."

"Oh, Hoong Wei, everyone likes to hear you play," said Mama. "*Ai ya!* Please, don't wiggle!" Mama was trying to wrap the red ribbons around Hoong Wei's pigtails. But no matter how hard she tried, Hoong Wei's hair would never lay in a neat braid like her older sister's. The stubborn pigtails always stuck out like little straw fans.

"But my playing is awful!" Hoong Wei persisted.

Mama smiled and gave Hoong Wei a reassuring squeeze.

"You and Hoong Yee always play beautifully." Then, tying the ribbons into bows, she said, "*Hao le!* Now, please go and say good morning to Popo."

Hoong Wei followed her older sister into the living room.

"*Zao!*" said Hoong Yee.

"*Zao!*" said Hoong Wei.

Their grandmother looked up from her chair and smiled at the two girls. "What a busy morning this is!" she said cheerily. "I must finish Hoong Wei's party jacket by tonight. *Ai ya*, all these loose buttons!"

Hoong Wei could never resist twisting and tugging at the round golden buttons, and now they dangled like the eyes of a Chinese New Year dragon.

"Popo," Hoong Wei began as she watched her grandmother's nimble fingers fasten a button, "when I play the piano in front of people, I make so many mistakes."

Popo put down her sewing and drew Hoong Wei close to her. "Don't you worry, *bao bei*. Everything will be fine tonight."

Still, Hoong Wei wished Popo would not finish sewing. Then she would get to wear her plain cotton jacket and no one would notice her and remember to ask her to play.

"Only one more button!" said Popo brightly.

Hoong Wei sighed loudly. So far, she was not feeling lucky at all.

"Hoong Yee, Hoong Wei! *Lai, lai, lai!*" called Mama from the kitchen. "Please come help!"

In the kitchen, tall stacks of bamboo steamers full of *ha gao* — small, plump shrimp dumplings — rattled merrily on the stove. Hoong Wei thought they sounded like the clattering of many mah-jongg tiles. Mama was busy stirring big iron woks filled with shredded meat and vegetables.

"Look, girls!" said Popo, taking a tray out of the oven. "*Yue bing!*"

"Mooncakes!" cried Hoong Yee.

"*Rabbit* mooncakes!" cried Hoong Wei.

Oh, Mama's mooncakes were beautiful! The little honey-colored cakes

were shaped like rabbits in honor of the Year of the Rabbit. Each one was carefully wrapped in a thin golden crust with curled edges, and each was filled with a rich, dark sweetness. With her eyes closed, Hoong Wei could almost taste the sweet sticky lotus-seed filling.

"Very, very hot!" cautioned Mama. She carefully placed the tray of cakes near the window to cool. Glancing at the kitchen clock, she said, "Hoong Yee, Hoong Wei, time to practice piano before company comes. Hoong Wei, please, first."

"*Zao gao!*" muttered Hoong Wei as she sat down at the piano. She glared at her music and began pecking out the melody of her Chinese poem song.

From the kitchen, Mama hummed along. Hoong Wei's fingers stumbled across the keys, and every time she turned the page, she lost her place.

When Hoong Yee took her turn, she didn't play a single wrong note.

"Don't you ever get nervous playing in front of people?" Hoong Wei asked crossly.

"Oh, Hoong Wei, you worry too much," said Hoong Yee.

Suddenly they heard a loud crash downstairs. Then the basement door creaked open, and Hoong Wei's father stepped out, carrying the mah-jongg table and chairs.

When he came back to the kitchen for a tea break, Hoong Wei was waiting for him. "Baba, who is coming tonight?"

"*Da jia*," answered Baba. "The whole family — including your favorite cousins, Meta and Hansen."

Hoong Wei liked Meta and Hansen, but her whole family was as big as her first-grade class! She looked up at her father and whispered, "Do I *have* to play the piano in front of so many people tonight, Baba? What if I lose my place or hit a wrong note?"

"Your Auntie Sum, if you remember," said Baba with a smile, "does not always sing the right notes, but everyone still likes to hear her sing."

Yes, I know, thought Hoong Wei. But with me, they will laugh.

The only thing to do, Hoong Wei decided, would be to stay out of sight in a quiet hiding place. Then the family would forget all about her!

Hoong Wei scurried down the dark basement stairs to look for a good place to hide. This would be perfect! It was dark and cool, and she could sit and eat mooncakes curled up in the old bean bag chair.

"Hoong Yee, Hoong Wei! *Fai di lai!*" called Mama from the kitchen. "The guests are here. Hoong Wei, come put on your party jacket."

Mama handed the girls a dish of preserved plums and a *cha hu* — a woven bamboo container filled with hot tea — to serve the arriving guests.

"*Nin hǎo?* How are you?" said Hoong Yee and Hoong Wei together as they bowed respectfully to their elder relatives. Mama and Baba watched proudly, then kissed the tops of their heads.

"Do you think we have the biggest family in the neighborhood?" Hoong Wei whispered to her sister. Every corner of the house was filling up with aunties, uncles, and cousins.

The evening darkened into night, and slowly the year's brightest moon rose to the highest point in the sky. Soon delicious smells from the kitchen made everyone very hungry.

"*Qing zuo! Qing zuo!*" announced Mama. "Please, come sit down. Dinner is served."

Mama looked beautiful, smiling in her new silk *qiong sam*. And what a wonderful feast she had prepared! Platters of Hoong Wei's favorite dishes filled the center of the large table — paper-thin scallion pancakes, mustard greens laced with oyster sauce, and *zong zi*, balls of sticky rice wrapped in dark green lotus leaves. Everything looks so delicious, thought Hoong Wei, and the best part — the rabbit mooncakes — is yet to come!

Hoong Yee, Hoong Wei, and their cousins happily settled at the children's table, where they ate and ate. Afterward, they built castles with milky-white mah-jongg tiles. Playing with Meta, Hansen, and her other cousins, Hoong Wei forgot about the piano.

But after all the dishes had been cleared and everyone came back to the living room for hot tea and oranges, Hoong Wei saw the piano rack filled with sheet music. This was the time Mama would ask her to play.

Hoong Wei felt her stomach muscles tighten. This was worse than roll call at school! Every morning, she would wait for her teacher to mispronounce her name in a bright, loud voice: "*Honey Why!*"

"Hoong Yee, Hoong Wei," called Mama when everyone was seated. "*Lai, lai, lai!*"

Hoong Wei looked at the door to the basement and began edging her way to her hiding place. Suddenly she felt a tug on her sleeve. She looked behind her. It was Hoong Yee.

"*Bai le!* Who wants to play in a silly piano recital!" whispered Hoong Yee. "Let's run away and hide in our crab apple tree!"

Hoong Wei couldn't believe her luck. Hoong Yee didn't want to play the piano either! So the lucky red ribbons had worked after all! Now they could escape together.

"Hoong Yee, Hoong Wei!" Mama called, and the two sisters giggled mischievously. "*Lai, lai, lai!* Hoong Yee, Hoong Wei!"

Out the back door they ran, the cool evening air rushing at their faces. Hoong Wei scampered up the crab apple tree and swung her legs over a branch. Finally, she and Hoong Yee were safe in their favorite place. Hoong Wei closed her eyes and hugged her knees happily.

Then, from the house, they heard someone playing a melody on the piano.

"Auntie Sum is playing your Chinese poem song," said Hoong Yee with a frown. "And she is singing off-key."

Before Hoong Wei could say a word, Hoong Yee was sliding down the trunk of the tree, dusting off her party jacket, and heading back to the house.

"What are you doing?" cried Hoong Wei.

"*Lai, lai, lai!*" Hoong Yee called out to her sister. "We can sing and play better than *that!* Come on!"

Oh, how could somebody be so lucky one minute and so unlucky the next? thought Hoong Wei. But she followed Hoong Yee and stood watching in the doorway as Auntie Sum stood up to make room for Hoong Yee on the piano bench.

Then Mama and Baba gave Hoong Wei such big smiles that she slowly made her way to the piano and sat down next to her sister.

The room fell quiet. All eyes were on Hoong Yee and Hoong Wei in their bright silk jackets with the round golden buttons. Softly they began to play. Mama joined in, singing in her clear, sweet voice:

By my bed, the moon shines bright

牀 前 明 月 光

And appears like icy foam.

疑 是 地 上 霜

I raise my head in moonbeams' light;

舉 頭 望 明 月

My head in hand, I long for home.

低 頭 思 故 鄉

As they reached the bottom of the first page, Hoong Wei's fingers slipped and she made a *very* loud mistake, which seemed to hang in the air. Hoong Wei's ears burned. Now everyone would start laughing.

But no one laughed. No one even seemed to notice! Only Hoong Yee, who quickly guided Hoong Wei to the next line, and Mama, who moved closer and began singing a little louder. From across the room, Auntie Sum joined in, her funny off-tune voice floating above the music.

By the third page, Hoong Wei felt much better. She sat up straighter on the piano bench. Suddenly, sitting here in the center of her big family, right next to Hoong Yee, seemed to Hoong Wei a very good place to be.

At the end of the final refrain, Hoong Wei looked up.

"*Hao ji le!*" she cried happily. "Look what Popo is bringing us!"

Into the living room came Popo, carrying a dessert tray. On it she had placed two beautiful rabbit mooncakes.

"Tonight," she said, "the first rabbit mooncakes are for our two little musicians, in gratitude for their lovely piano music."

Everyone clapped and cheered. Hoong Wei stood next to Hoong Yee, smiling from ear to ear.

After Mama served dessert to the rest of the family, Baba lifted his glass and made the first good luck toast to the Harvest Moon. "May the Harvest Moon bless us with good fortune and bring our family together on this night each year."

Hoong Wei whispered her own toast. "*Xie xie nin.* Thank you, bright moon."

Good luck, she decided, had been with her all along.

And outside, the Harvest Moon, the fullest and most glorious moon of the year, shone softly throughout the night.